RUM-A-TUM-TUM

by Angela Shelf Medearis

illustrated by James E. Ransome

Holiday House/New York

To Coleen Salley, with love from both of us.
Your New Orleans accent, funny stories, and personal tour
of the city made this book come alive.

A.S.M. and J.E.R.

Text copyright © 1997 by Angela Shelf Medearis
Illustrations copyright © 1997 by James E. Ransome
ALL RIGHTS RESERVED
Printed in the United States of America
FIRST EDITION

Library of Congress Cataloging-in-Publication Data
Medearis, Angela Shelf, 1956–
Rum-a-tum-tum / Angela Shelf Medearis: illustrated by James E.
Ransome. — 1st ed.
p.   cm.
Summary: Describes all the different sounds one can hear
on Market Street.
ISBN 0-8234-1143-5
[1. Sound—Fiction.   2. Neighborhood—Fiction.   3. Stories in
rhyme.]   I. Ransome, James E., ill.   II. Title.
PZ8.3.M551155Ru   1997   94-9929   CIP   AC
[E]—dc20

Bananas! Bananas!
I'm your banana man!
Lady, lady,
bring your dishpan!

Every morning when I open my eyes,
my ears wake up to street vendors' cries.
I run to the window, open it wide,
lean over the railing and look outside.

Nice little snap beans,
pretty little corn,
butter beans, carrots,
jui-cy lemons!

I see baskets of pears and yellow bananas,
Creole women in red bandannas,
wobbly wagons and a rickety cart.
My morning is off to a noisy start.

I got strawberries, lady!
Two baskets for a quarter!
Blackberries, blueberries,
come and place your order!

Shouting vendors with baskets on heads
wake up sleepers still in their beds.
Doors fly open and neighbors spill out
to see what the noise is all about.

Okra, cucumbers,
squash and potatoes,
come and sample
my plump tomatoes.

Momma's outside with baskets in hand
to buy green beans from the vegetable stand.
She sniffs, squeezes, and pokes each pile,
"Nice tomatoes," she says with a smile.

Juicy red watermelons!
So sweet and fine!
Eat the meat, pickle the rind,
save the seeds till planting time!

"Buy from me," the fruit vendors shout
  as shoppers bustle in and out.
"Ripe, fresh melons, sweet as honey.
  Lots of fruit for a little money."

Crayfish, oysters,
flounder on ice,
fry them, boil them,
serve them up nice!

Slippery fish with sightless eyes
stare at shoppers searching for buys.
"Two pounds of shrimp," says Mrs. Lee.
"When I close my eyes, I smell the sea!"

Red apples! Green apples!
Apples for pie!
Sweet apples, sour apples,
come out and buy!

Dressing quickly, I run downstairs
to buy an apple and two sweet pears.

I sit outside and eat my treat.
All grows quiet on Market Street.

Nearer my God to thee,
nearer to thee,
nearer my God to thee,
nearer to thee.

Black-plumed horses pass me by.
Black-clad mourners wail and cry,
softly moaning a sorrowful song
as sadly, slowly they move along.

Chimney sweep, chimney sweep,
brush away that soot and dirt.
Sweep 'em clean! Sweep 'em clean!
Save the fireman lots of work.

Chimney sweeps in stovepipe hats
cross the roof like frock-tailed cats.
Acrobats on roofs so high,
sooty silhouettes against the sky.

RUM-A-TUM-TUM, RUM-A-TUM-TUM.

Boom, boom, boom roar the big red drums.
Look, a parade! Here it comes!

High-stepping, sharp-dressing men in a row
blowing hot jazz notes wherever they go.

RUM-A-TUM-TUM, RUM-A-TUM-TUM,
RUM-A-TUM-TUM-TUM-TUM.

Costumed revelers make a din!
Rum-a-tum-tum, grab hands, join in.
Faces shiny with summertime heat
whirl and twirl to the magic beat.

RUM-A-TUM-TUM, RUM-A-TUM-TUM,
RUM-A-TUM-TUM-TUM-TUM.

I sing and sway, I feel so fine,
finger-snapping, toe-tapping in a line.
I clap my hands and stomp my feet,
dancing along to the song of the street.

RUM-A-TUM-TUM, RUM-A-TUM-TUM,
RUM-A-TUM-TUM-TUM-TUM.

AUTHOR'S NOTE

I was in the library doing some research on New Orleans in the early 1900s, and I discovered a collection of "street cries." Street cries are the poetic advertisements salespeople all over America used before the invention of television and radio. Peddlers traveled up and down the streets selling their wares in a sing-song voice. Each vendor had a melodious "cry" that was his or her trademark.

As I did more research, I could imagine the lively, colorful, noisy streets of New Orleans in the early morning. Later, I met Gwen Brisco and Ferdinand Bigard, both of whom had been born and raised in New Orleans. Gwen told me about sitting on her front steps and watching the exciting things that happened every day on her street and joining in the "second line" dancing whenever there was a parade. Ferdinand had been a street vendor's helper as a child. He sang out his street cry for me over the telephone. *Rum-a-Tum-Tum* is based on the street cries of old and the wonderful memories of early life in New Orleans relayed to me by Ms. Brisco and Mr. Bigard.

—A.S.M.